This book is dedicated to my nieces and nephews and to
my future children, if I get that chance. May you know that
God, your Heavenly Father, hears your prayers and loves
you. When you want to talk to Him, you can kneel by your
bed, take a walk in nature, or simply close your eyes to take
a moment inside of you to say what's on your heart to Him.
He'll hear you and let you know He's there for you. —D. A.

**BUSHEL
& PECK
BOOKS**

Text copyright © 2021 by David Archuleta.
Illustration copyright © 2021 by Sara Ugolotti.

Published by Bushel & Peck Books, a family-run publishing house in Fresno, California, who
believes in uplifting children with the highest standards of art, music, literature, and ideas.
Find beautiful books for gifted young minds at www.bushelandpeckbooks.com.

Type set in Providence Sans Pro, Josefin Sans, and Braisetto.

Bushel & Peck Books is dedicated to fighting illiteracy all over the world. For every book we
sell, we donate one to a child in need—book for book. To nominate a school or organization to
receive free books, please visit www.bushelandpeckbooks.com.

LCCN: 2021937454
ISBN: 9781952239540

First Edition

Printed in China

10 9 8 7 6 5 4 3 2 1

My Little Prayer

SOCCER
TRYOUTS
MONDAY!

DAVID
ARCHULETA

ILLUSTRATED BY
SARA UGOLOTTI

Heavenly Father, I am grateful
for your eternal presence.

I am learning to be patient
and that you are really there.

Sometimes I am afraid,

and I know that's lacking faith.

But I'm beginning to understand
that for me you have a plan.

Heavenly Father, I am grateful
for you sending your Son . . .

. . . to die so that I'd live . . .

. . . and for never giving up.

I'm learning everyday
that I won't always have my way.

But I'm beginning to understand

that for me you have a plan.

Heavenly Father, I am grateful for you hearing my prayer.

I am learning to be patient
and that you are really there.

There are answers I'm receiving;

no, they're not
always immediate.

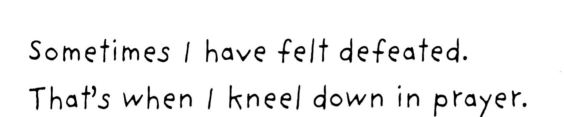

Sometimes I have felt defeated.
That's when I kneel down in prayer.

You've shown me you hear my prayer.
I'm amazed by how you care,
'cause you hear . . .

... my little prayer.